EVERLASTING
Tales of
Vikram & Betal

Everlasting Tales of Vikram & Betal

ISBN 81-8388-170-X

Published in 2007 by

SPIDER BOOKS
AH-73/1, 7th Main Road, Shanthi Colony
Anna Nagar, Chennai - 600 040 (INDIA)
Phone: 044-42171048 / 32934340
E-mail: spider@spiderbooks.net

Written by
Almas Viquar
Illustrations
V.K.Santhosh

Printed in India

CONTENTS

CONTENTS

The Sage And The Fruit

Many years ago, there was a King called Vikramaditya. He ruled over a city on the banks of the river Godavari. He was very famous for his bravery and courage. People of his kingdom loved him for his wisdom and justice.

Everyday, King Vikram would attend the proceedings in his royal court. People from his kingdom and the neighbouring towns would visit him with their woes and he would do great justice to them. The people would be hugely rewarded for their goodness in his court. King Vikramaditya was not only courageous but also had a flair for learning and adventure.

One day, when King Vikram was in court listening to his people, a sage came to the court. Vikramaditya greeted him cheerfully. The sage presented him a fruit and said, "O King, please

The sage and the fruit

accept this humble gift from me. This gift denotes my admiration and love for you." The king was very pleased. "It is my honour to be gifted by you. I accept this with love, O Sage. I will treasure this gift of yours till my last breath," said the pleased king. The sage took leave. The king handed the fruit to his treasurer and said, "Like all the other treasures, this fruit also should be kept in the treasury, for this belongs to the people of my kingdom."

This became a daily habit. Everyday, the Sage would visit the king's court and presented him a fruit. Days passed, the king collected many fruits of that sort from the hermit and treasured it along with the diamonds and emeralds. The king could not understand as to why the sage presented a fruit to him everyday. But still, he did not know the reason for this. However, one morning, Vikram noticed a monkey sitting on the palace wall.

As he was taking the fruit to give it to the treasurer, the monkey grabbed it from his hand and started eating the fruit. Suddenly a dazzling gem fell out of it. The king was very surprised. He immediately ordered his treasurer to get him all the fruits kept in the storage. The fruits had got rotten but when the king had them all crushed, each one of them yielded a precious gem. The king then had them examined and they all were the finest gems. The king wondered, "What did the sage want to convey with these gems. What does he want in return for this wonderful and priceless gift?"

The king then distributed all those precious stones to the poor. King Vikram was not able to sleep the whole night, was very puzzled.

Next morning, the sage came to the court at his usual time with yet another fruit. On

seeing the sage, King Vikram welcomed him. Vikram very eager asked him politely, "Your holiness, Can you please tell me why you have been giving me such precious stones? Without good reason, I cannot accept any gifts from you." The sage replied, "I need the help of a brave man for a spiritual goal. For this spiritual prayers to perform, a courageous man is required. And I can't see a more daring and brave man like you, O' King in this entire kingdom." He continued, "I also know you would not let me down." Vikram readily agreed to this. So the Sage said, "O' King! Please come to the burial ground on the next moonless night. It is at a distance of forty miles from here. I will wait for you under a banyan tree." Vikram agreed to carry out these instructions.

On the said night, King Vikram covered his head and body with a black cloth. Kept on walking towards the burial ground. It was very dark and he was only able to see the eyes of the owls staring at him. There was only ghostly silence around him. As he neared the burial ground in the forest, he heard the noises of wild animals. Without getting scared, he moved forward. When he reached the spot, he saw the sage waiting for him. The king asked the sage as to what he can do to help him.

The sage replied, "King Vikram! To the south of this forest is an old tamarind tree on which hangs a corpse upside down. But it is possessed by an evil spirit called Betal. Please bring it to me. On that corpse, I need to perform the spiritual rites to bring peace and harmony among the people of this kingdom. This job requires a lot of courage and I have all the faith in you, O' King."

The king immediately followed the sage's orders and reached the tamarind tree. There he saw the corpse hanging from a branch, upside down.

On finding the corpse there, he took his sword and cut the branches on which the corpse had been tied to the branch. The corpse fell to the ground and laughed loudly. The king realised that it was a ghost. But the courageous king carried the body over his shoulders and started towards his kingdom. A short distance later, the ghost left Vikram's shoulders and escaped to its original spot. The king climbed up the tree, brought down the ghost and placing it on his shoulders started walking again. "Who are you?" he asked the ghost. "I am Betal" replied the ghost and in turn he said, "Vikram, I heard a lot about your courage and wisdom and now I witnessed your courage. Where are you taking me? O' King." The king replied, "A sage has requested me to bring you to him."

Betal did not have any objection to going with Vikram but he laid down a condition, "We have to cover a long distance and to relieve the tedious walk, I will tell you a story. But you should not utter even one word till we reach the destination. If by chance, you utter anything, I will fly back to the tamarind tree and hang by it. Do you agree to this?" asked Betal.

The king, being very sensible kept listening to Betal, not uttering a word. Betal said, "I will narrate a story to you so that you do not feel the strain of walking. At the end of each story, there will be a puzzle. With your knowledge of wisdom, you should solve the puzzle. Listen to the story carefully and answer me. Knowing the answers, if you do not reply, your head will be shattered into a thousand pieces. Beware!"

The spirit then started narrating the story.

Noble Sacrifice

A king named Devendra ruled the kingdom of Suryansh. He was very powerful and righteous in his manner of giving justice. He had issued an order that no man could have more than one wife and nobody could marry some other person's wife. Anybody found guilt was to be punished.

A young man named Dhananjay lived in the kingdom of Suryansh. He was a very wealthy man. He had acquired a lot of wealth and properties through his ancestors. Dhananjay was a bachelor. His parents started looking for a beautiful bride for their son. One evening, as Dhananjay was taking a stroll in the city, he met an extremely beautiful girl. At the very first sight, Dhananjay fell in love with her and decided to marry her.

On reaching home, Dhananjay called for his friend. He asked his friend to find out where the girl lived and what was her name. His friend returned a few days later with the information about the girl. Her name was Chandrika and she was the daughter of another rich merchant Malayaketu of the same city.

Dhananjay sent the same friend to Malayaketu's house with the marriage proposal. But by that time, Malayaketu had already fixed up his daughter's marriage to a man called Jayachandra. When he heard of this, Dhananjay was very upset. He himself went to the merchant's house and said, "O' noble man, I ask for your daughter's hand in marriage, if you find me suitable." The merchant replied, "You are indeed worthy, O young man. But you are too late as I have fixed Chandrika's marriage with

another man." Dhananjay took leave of the merchant with a heavy heart. Having loved Chandrika very deeply, he decided not even to think of marriage with any other girl. When Chandrika heard of Dhananjay's love for her, she felt sorry for him. She went to Dhananjay's house to say that she had to abide by her father's decision. She developed a soft corner for Dhananjay. She also started to like him. She thought that how cruel the life is to her. "How I wish to marry the handsome young Dhananjay," sighed Chandrika. She silently accepted her father's choice.

Chandrika's marriage with Jayachandra was a grand affair. She was a very honest girl. So, when she was alone with her husband, without hiding anything, she told Jayachandra about Dhananjay and her love for him. Pleased with her honesty, her husband allowed her to meet Dhananjay as he felt he should not come in between the two ardent lovers. That same night, she left the house of Jayachandra and walked towards Dhananjay's place, through a thick forest. She was very scared of the darkness and kept walking. As she feared, on her way, a thief suddenly jumped out of the bushes. He wanted to rob her of all her jewellery. Chandrika pleaded with him, "Please let me go now. I promise you that I will hand over the jewellery on my way back." The thief took pity on her, believed her and allowed her to proceed.

It was very dark. Chandrika hurried off towards Dhananjay's house. He was shocked to see Chandrika standing in front of him. He got angry and scolded her, "How can a girl and that too, a married girl come to me at such a late hour? Go back to your husband, Chandrika. This is not a right thing to do and moreover don't you know the king's order? It is an offence on

our part to meet like this. If he sees us now, he will impose death penalty on us."

Stunned by Dhananjay's attitude, Chandrika at once left the place. She kept crying as she did not expect this from her love, Dhananjay. She started back to her husband's house. Tears rolled down her face. On her way back, she met the thief who had been waiting for her. The thief was pleased to see Chandrika and that she had kept her promise. "Now, young lady, give me all your jewels as you had promised," said the thief. As he came nearer to Chandrika, he saw her sad face. The thief got curious and asked Chandrika, "What is the matter? Why are you looking so sad? Then Chandrika narrated her story to the thief. The thief took pity on her and told her, "You are very honest. I will not steal anything from you. Instead, I will escort you to your house."

Chandrika reached home and told her husband about what transpired between herself and Dhananjay. But Jayachandra did not believe her. "My doors are closed for you. I left it to your choice and you chose to leave my place. Now there is no place for you in my heart. You shall leave my house at once," said Jayachandra and slammed the door in the face of Chandrika. She had nowhere to go. Feeling distressed and helpless, she committed suicide.

Betal ended his narration here and asked Vikram, "You have heard the story with apt attention. Now, decide and tell me immediately, who is the most noble of these four persons. Who made the noble sacrifice among them. Was it Chandrika who ended her life? Or was it her husband who had agreed to send her to Dhananjay? Or the thief, who without robbing her, sent her away? Or was it Dhananjay who wanted Chandrika to go back to her husband? If you know the answer and still prefer to remain quiet, your head will split into pieces. Beware!"

Vikram immediately answered, "Betal! A sacrifice made without selfish motives is the greatest sacrifice. In this story, Chandrika took an extreme step by ending her life because she got herself in an awkward situation and had no place to go to. Dhananjay did not accept Chandrika fearing the king's punishment. And her husband gave up his wife because she was never his and doubted her and did not want her. All these had selfish motives."

Vikram explained, "Only the thief made a true sacrifice. He was the most noble of these four persons. He could have easily robbed her but let her go without any selfishness on his part."

"Vikram," said Betal, "I like your judgement. But you have spoken, so I am going back to the tree." Saying so, Betal flew back to the tree. Since Vikram was determined to hand over Betal to the sage, he dashed towards the tree.

The Delicate Queens

Even without a bit o frustration, King Vikram reached the tree on which the spirit resided in a corpse hanging upside down from the tree's branch. As he started waking towards the cemetery after hoisting Betl on his shoulder, the spirit spoke through the lead man's lips, "O' valiant King, to my mind, cones the story of a King called Yashketu. I vill narrate to you the story."

Long ago, King Yashketu ruled Nepal. He had three wives. He loved them all anche treated them well. One evening the king vas taking a walk in the garden with one of is queens, Mayavathi. She had worn a flowe in her hair. Due to gentle breeze blowing in e garden, the flower from her hair fell and it her thigh. "Ouch!" she screamed. This h caused her a wound. Unable to bear the pa, Queen Mayavathi fainted.

The delicate queens

The king at once carried her to the royal palace and had her wound treated. The king was shocked to see that the falling of a flower on her thigh had bruised her. The king said surprisingly, "How delicate my queen is."

Few days passed. One night, the king was sleeping in the royal bedroom, along with his second wife, Taramathi. It was a full moon night. Suddenly he heard Taramathi scream with pain. He rushed towards her to see what had happened and what made the queen scream with pain. He saw that the rays of the moon reaching through the window had burnt her body and limbs.

The king got very frightened when he saw burn marks all over Taramathi's body. She was crying in pain as if the rays of the moon were red hot. "I can't bear it, O king," cried the queen. Instantly, the king ordered the maid to take care of the queen and called for the

royal physician to attend to her. He also ordered the maids to lay Taramathi on lotus leaves and to smear sandalwood paste on her burns.

The king was very worried and he was not able to sleep the whole night thinking about his wives. The next morning, the king summoned his third wife Chandrakala to his chamber. To reach the room she had to walk through a corridor. While she was walking on the thickly carpeted corridor, she heard the sound of rice being pounded. "My God! I cannot tolerate the noise, please for God's sake, stop this noise. Ah… I cannot bear it anymore." She cried out, closing her ears with her palms and few minutes later, she collapsed on the floor.

The king came running to the corridor where queen Chandrakala was lying unconscious on the floor. He was shocked to

find blisters on both her palms. They looked red and swollen as if she was pounding rice all her life. The king then instructed the maids to apply some soothing lotion on Chandrakala's palms and ordered the maids to be with her till she gets better.

Thinking about the delicate nature of his queens, the king had to spend the night alone.

Betal ended the story and teased king Vikram, "O' Handsome King! You also have several queens. If you were also to face a similar situation, whom would you consider as the most delicate and sensitive one. Look Vikram, I warn you! do not keep quiet."

Vikram was getting fed up of Betal's tactics. If he were to talk, Betal did the disappearing act. Otherwise, he himself faced death.

Since Vikram knew the answer, he did not want to remain silent and be dead. So he answered Betal thus, "Of the three queens, Chandrakala has the most delicate skin and she is the daintiest." But none have heard about the rays of the moon causing the burns or about a flower causing wounds" argued Betal. "Yes, these two other queens also had very delicate skin," admitted Vikram. "But the moon's rays and the flower touched their skin directly and they were unable to bear the pain."

"Where as, Queen Chandrakala developed blisters just by hearing the sound of rice-pounding and that too at a distance. So she had the most delicate and the most sensitive skin", was his reasoning.

"You amaze me with your logical thinking" complimented Betal. Since the king opened his mouth, Betal flew back to the tamarind tree.

Madhumalathi

Yet once again, King Vikram returned to the tree at midnight, brought down Betal, hoisted it onto his shoulder and without uttering a word, started walking. As he kept walking, Betal started speaking.

"O King of Kings, it amazes me to witness your determination to complete the job, you have taken up. Nothing is stopping you, as there is horror and darkness surrounding you. It is true that a determined effort is what leads to fulfilment of a task." After praising the King, Betal started narrating a story.

There, once lived a Brahmin called Surendra in a town on the banks of Yamuna river. He was a great scholar. He had an extremely beautiful daughter. Her name was Madhumalathi.

When Madhumalathi attained the age of marriage, Surendra wanted an ideal husband for her. All the eligible bachelors of the town wanted to marry the heavenly beauty, Madhumalathi. Surendra started searching for a handsome, intelligent and well-mannered boy who suits his daughter's immense beauty.

People of the town came to know that Surendra was searching for an alliance for his daughter. A few weeks later, three boys hailing from different towns visited the Surendra's house. All of them were handsome and intelligent. Each one of them had seen the girl at a fair and were enchanted by her beauty. They all felt that they would willingly end their lives for the sake of Madhumathi. They approached Surendra and requested for Madhumalathi's hand in marriage. Surendra was really very confused. Neither he nor his wife could decide upon any of these three

young men. They wanted their daughter to take the decision as she had to spend all her life with the man she was to marry.

Even Madhumalathi found it difficult to decide whom to wed. On an auspicious day, Surendra invited the three suitors to his house so that his daughter could choose her husband. But since all the three young men were equally good-looking and intelligent, the girl also found it difficult.

When Madhumalathi was sitting in her room thinking about her decision, a snake suddenly entered the room and bit her. Unfortunately, she died. Her young suitors were extremely grieved and depressed.

The three young men had loved Madhumalathi very deeply and so, they decided to spend the rest of their lives in her memory.

After Madhumalathi's cremation was over, one of the suitor's collected some of her ashes, immersed them in the river Ganges and started to live close by.

The second one built a hut at the place where the cremation took place and spread the ashes, using it as a bed. The third one roamed from one holy place to another. He looked shabby, only thinking of Madhumalathi's grace and beauty. During one such trips, he happened to stay overnight with a tantrik. That night, the tantrik's son came running towards the Yagna fire, and suddenly the little boy lost his balance and fell into the fire. Before anybody realised what had happened, the boy turned into ashes. The tantrik's wife started crying and howling, "My only son turned into ashes, I want my son back. Please get him back for me," She pleaded with the tantrik. The tantrik, then consoled his wife and began

to chant some prayers before the boys ashes. The tantrik took some mud from the ground and sprinkled it over the boy's dead body. Amazingly, the little boy came back to life.

The third suitor, who was watching all this, was very thrilled. "That way even Madhumalathi can come back to life!" he thought. Fortunately for him, he remembered the prayers which the tantrik offered on the ashes. So he hurried back to the banks of Ganges where Madhumalathi was cremated. On reaching there, he met the other two young men. He told them all that he had seen and how he could get back the life of Madhumalathi. They were very happy at the thought of seeing Madhumalathi alive.

The second suitor then ran into his hut and brought the pot of Madhumalathi's ashes. The third suitor who knew the verses, recited the prayers, and the other suitor sprinkled some holy water on the ashes. The magic worked and Madhumalathi stood up from the ashes, more beautiful than ever before. The three young men were very thrilled.

But then, the question arises as to who would marry the pretty girl. They started fighting with each other, claiming her as his own. One suitor claimed, "It is me who chanted the prayer. That's why she got back her life." Another said, "She only belongs to me as I had preserved the ashes of Madhumalathi all these years. Otherwise how could she have become alive?" The third one declared, "After all, I only sprinkled the holy water on her and gave her a new life. So, Madhumalathi has to be my wife."

Betal ended his story here and asked Vikram "O King, you have heard the story. Now tell me how would you resolve this. Who do you think is the right suitor for

Madhumalathi? If you know the answer and still do not reply to me, your head will burst into pieces." Betal said very sarcastically, "I know you know the answer. So answer me O King."

Vikram very calmly answered, "The young man who gave her life by reciting the prayer will be like a father to her. The suitor who immersed her ashes in the river behaved like a son. That's a very sacred relationship. The young man who actually renounced everything and had her ashes preserved, acted like a true beloved. And so he is the right suitor for her."

"Your wisdom is unbelievable, O King. You are as usual right," praised Betal. "But since you have spoken I shall return to the tamarind tree."

The Brahmin And His Sons

Betal watched from the corner of his eyes, as King Vikram neared the tree where it was hung upside down from the tree's branch. It remained silent as King Vikram brought down the corpse and started walking. Betal started to speak, "O King, seeing you perform such a task in the dark of the night, when people would hesitate to do so even during day time, makes me wonder that how dedicated you are to your job assigned, by the Sage. Let me tell you a story. Listen to the whole story. That way, you will not feel the strain of walking." The spirit then started narrating the story.

Once upon a time, there lived a wise Brahmin by name Sridhara in a city called Saharanpur. He had three foolish sons. The three boys, when young never took interest in studies and they learned nothing. They all spent their time fooling people and did nothing worthy to themselves or to their father. They did not even realise that they had grown up to be useless. The three of them were gamblers and loafers. All this time, the Brahmin took care of their needs but as time passed by, Sridhara became very weak and old. He was very worried for his sons. Sridhara decided to advise them. One day, he called all his sons and said, "My dear sons, I am worried about you all! What will happen to you when I am dead? Who will take care of your needs. Be sensible, sons. Loafers and corrupt people do not earn respect from anybody. Please forsake these sinful practices. Be of good character and lead a worthy life." Sridhara had a word of advice for them, "My dear children, earn knowledge, otherwise you will repent in your old age." His sons got some sense from their old father.

All the three sons paid heed to their father's advice and decided to lead a better life. They realised that lack of knowledge was a curse. So they decided to seek education and thereby earn their livelihood.

The next day, they set out in search of seeking knowledge. On their way, they met a stranger who told them about a teacher living in the nearby forest and who could teach them all the education and knowledge they wanted to learn. They lived with the teacher in his Gurukul for a couple of years and learnt the art of magic and the traditional subjects. They had acquired some amazing skills from their teacher and they decided to return to their hometown.

On their way back home, the three boys had to cross a dense forest. When they reached the middle of the forest, they saw a hunter shooting down a lion. They quickly went behind the bushes and hid themselves. The hunter after shooting the lion, separated the bones and skin of the lion and filled them in two separate sacks. The boys waited and watched. As it was getting darker, the hunter said to himself, "I will leave these sacks here and take it in the morning when it is bright and sunny." Saying that, the hunter left those sacks on the ground and left the place. On seeing the hunter leaving, they quickly jumped out of the bushes." "This is a very good opportunity", said one of the boy. "Let's test what we have learnt", said another. They all agreed. They began to remove the bones and the skin of the lion from the sack. They wanted to experiment what they had learnt with the help of the special skill gained from the teacher. The eldest brother arranged all the bones so as to resemble the structure of a lion's body. The lion's skeleton was ready. The second one used his magical powers to

provide flesh and skin over the skeleton. The creation looked strong and sturdy, but it was lifeless. "How harmless it looks without the life", said the third brother. He chanted some magic words and gave life to the lifeless lion. The ferocious lion rose up alive, roaring fiercely, pounced on the three brothers. Before they could act, the lion killed them tearing their limbs apart. They had indeed acquired knowledge, but they felt short of being wise. Their foolishness served them as their death trap. Within minutes, the three fools met their end.

Betal ended his narration at this stage. He asked the king, "Vikram! you are a highly intelligent person. Now tell me who is the stupidest of these brothers?" Betal quickly added his warning also, "If you know the answer and still keep quiet, your head will shatter into pieces."

Vikram could not possibly remain silent because he knows the answer. He therefore, replied, "The brother who filled the lion with life is the most foolish of them all. Inspite of his skills, he did not have the common sense to know that a living lion could be dangerous to their life. Only a fool will bring back a dead lion to life."

"You always amaze me with your knowledge, Vikram. But you have a bad habit of opening your mouth and so you lose me." said the Betal. Betal sprang out of his grasp and was back at the tamarind tree.

Vikram had no other alternative than to run after Betal.

The Sage Who Turned Into A Boy

Vikram was a man of enormous determination. Even after being tricked by Betal into talking many times, he went back to the tamarind tree and without losing patience, brought down the corpse, which was hanging upside down. Pulling down Betal from the branches, Vikram walked with firm steps.

Betal tried to dissuade Vikram about taking him to the sage. Vikram remained silent. So, to ease the boredom of the tedious journey, Betal had a story to tell.

Once, there lived a brahmin by name Prabhudev in the city of Jagatpur. He was a well-learned scholar. He had all the happiness in the world, a loving wife, enough wealth and an immensely big house to stay. The people of the city had a great respect for him

for his immense knowledge. But, he and his wife were always worried because they did not have children. "Who will look after us, as we grow old?" Said Prabhudev with a heavy heart.

After many years, their prayers were answered. By God's grace, a son was born to him in their old age. The boy was named as Sukhveer. The boy, when born, was of a very frail health. Sukhveer got the best of education, the brahmin and his wife loved their only son dearly. He grew up to be an intelligent young man. But bad luck struck on them. Sukhveer died of an infectious fever.

The brahmin and his wife could not control themselves on seeing Sukhveer dead. Prabhudev mourned the death of his son very much. He grieved over the fact that death had snatched away a young life while he himself was hale and hearty even in old age.

His relatives tried to console him. But the old brahmin just couldn't agree to the fact that his only son is dead and the body is kept in front of him. He became hysterical. He cried and cried even when the body was about to be cremated. "How cruel can life be," cried the brahmin.

An old sage was meditating in the crematorium at that time. He heard Prabhudev and his wife crying and wailing over their son's dead body. The sage got curious and wanted to know what had happened. "There are so many people and who is that wailing so loudly," murmured the sage. He sent one of his pupil to find out what had happened. The pupil returned to the sage with the information. The sage felt sorry for the brahmin and his wife.

The sage was a very old man. He had no strength even to walk by himself. Even then,

with great difficulty he reached the spot where the boy was to be cremated.

The sage looked at the young man's dead body and quickly thought of a trick to perform. The sage realised that it was a body of a young person. He wanted to get into the body himself with his divine powers.

He went close to the place where Sukhveer's body was kept. First, he cried bitterly. Then he laughed aloud. Then laughing and dancing, he discarded his old body with the help of the power he had and entered the dead body of the young lad.

And suddenly, Sukhveer's body showed signs of movement. Moments later, he sat up as if he had just come out of sleep. The entire gathering was very happy to see Sukhveer alive. More so, the brahmin and his wife. "It's a miracle. God has answered our prayers. He cannot see us childless," cried the brahmin's wife. They did not know what had actually happened but they were happy to have their son breathing again.

The sage talking through Sukhveer's body, told this father, "I had been to heaven. There, God made me take a vow. I fulfilled the vow and got back my life." He then asked the people gathered there to disperse.

After all of them left, the sage destroyed his old body and enjoyed life as Sukhveer, the young man.

Betal ended the story at this stage and asked the king, "Vikram! Why did the sage cry at first? Why did he sing and dance later? I warn you, not to keep silent."

Vikram was fed up with Betal's questions. He thought that by answering Betal this time, he would make him obedient. Moreover, if he kept quiet, death was sure to him. With no other option, Vikram answered Betal.

"Betal! the sage was a very old man. Throughout his life, he had strived hard to attain the divine powers. That's why he cried as he had to discard his old body and his own identity. At the same time, he felt very happy that he could, having a youthful body, live much longer than expected. After all, everybody likes to be young."

Betal agreed with Vikram. But he found another opportunity to slip out of Vikram's hands. Hanging demonically, he shouted," Vikram! you have talked, Vikram! you have talked" and disappeared into the tamarind tree.

The Faithful Minister

Even though, King Vikram believed in the power of the spirit's curse, with the greater belief that he could escape it, he reached the tree yet again, brought down Betal from its branch, carried it on his shoulder and without uttering a word, started walking in a dedicated manner.

As always, Betal started speaking, "O King, even in this pitch dark night, at a time when vicious animals wander about, and despite having failed many times, if you are returning to this cemetery so patiently, one has to definitely praise you for your perseverance. If, by chance, you succeed in this attempt of yours, I will be the first one to praise you. To reduce the hardship of your chosen path, let me tell you another story."

Once there lived a king called Rajdheer who ruled over Pataliputra. Loved dearly by the citizens of Pataliputra, the king had won

the hearts and respect of all his subjects. Other kings ruled their kingdoms, keeping in mind Rajdheer as their role model. But there was emptiness in his life as he was unmarried. He started looking for a bride for himself .He made an announcement to the people that he was looking for a girl to wed. "Whoever's daughter is eligible for marriage shall inform the king. If the king finds the girl suitable, he would make her his queen," was the announcement made by his men throughout the kingdom.

All the people who had daughters of marriageable age wanted their daughters to be married to the king. "Start to dress up well and groom yourself to be liked by the king," said one of the father to his daughter. "How lucky will my daughter be if the king marries her" said an other father.

In the same kingdom, lived a rich merchant called Keshav who had a very beautiful and charming daughter. She was called Padmavathi. If people of this kingdom talk of beauty, they gave examples of Padmavathi. She was not only beautiful but also a very intelligent young girl. "Padmavathi has grown up and is eligible for marriage now," her mother told Keshav. And so, as per the king's order, Keshav went to inform the king about this.

"There are many other proposals along with this one. Give me some time, O humble man. If I find your daughter suitable, I shall marry her, otherwise, you can get her married to one of my ministers. I will let you know in a few days time," said the king. The merchant took leave. On his way back home, he was thinking of his beautiful daughter's marriage with the king. He felt very happy on the thought of this.

The king then called out for his minister who happened to be the king's friend. The

minister was known to be wise at judging beauty and intelligence. "Here is one task for you, my friend. Go and test the merchant Keshav's daughter. Come and tell me if she is capable of becoming my queen. Remember, the girl has to have all the qualities which a queen requires and you know what I want," ordered the king to his minister.

The minister went to Keshav's house in disguise and met Padmavathi. He found her extremely beautiful and charming. He thought, "She looks so stunning, as if she has descended from the sky, like a Goddess." He was spell bound. But after spending sometime there in her house, he found her to be very bold and outspoken. "She may turn out to be too strong-willed. It is very possible that she would even dominate our king and interfere in his royal proceedings," thought the minister. So, the minister went to the king and told him that Padmavathi was not fit to become his queen. The king then arranged Padmavathi's marriage with one of his ministers.

A year passed. One day, the king was taking a stroll in the city. Accidentally, at that time Padmavathi was standing on the balcony of her house. The king had a glimpse of her and came to know that she was Padmavathi who the king was supposed to get married. He was stunned by her unmatched beauty and charm. "She looks like a Goddess from heaven. What bad luck that I refused her proposal," regretted Rajdheer. "How can the minister report that Padmavathi was unfit for me?" he thought.

King Rajdheer was not able to sleep that night thinking of Padmavathi. "What a grave mistake I made by getting her married to someone else," thought Rajdheer. He got really wild with his minister. On getting very angry, the king sentenced the minister to death, the very next day.

Betal ended the story and asked king Vikram, "Tell me, O King! you also give justice and punish the wrong doers. Was King Rajdheer justified in putting his minister to death?" "Not at all," came the reply from King Vikram." The minister was truly honest and faithful. He was loyal to his king by saying that Padmavathi was unfit for the king to wed. He was only concerned with the king and the kingdom's future. Therefore, what the minister did was right. King Rajdheer was unjustified in putting his faithful minister to death."

"Your logical thinking amazes me, Vikram and you are absolutely right," smiled Betal. "Indeed, unlike King Rajdheer you are the most wise and just king I have ever met. But only the bad thing is that you have broken your silence again and so I have to go." Saying this, Betal flew back. And King Vikram turned around and started following him...

Cost of Life

Recalling the promise made to the sage to hand over the corpse to him, Vikram followed Betal again and reached the tamarind tree. Vikram brought down Betal, mounted him on his shoulders and set out. Betal, as usual, dragged him into conversation. "O King, you are very determined in your task. You have come for me again. I will narrate to you a story, so that you do not feel the strain of carrying me," said Betal and started narrating the story without his usual warning. This surprised the king and caused him to listen to the story with attention.

A long time ago, a very noble and generous king ruled over a city called Vijayapura. Being an intelligent and wise person, he conducted his royal court proceedings listening to the grievances of his

subjects and solving their problem in a just manner without causing displeasure to his citizens.

Once, on old man came to the court of the king. He had brought his two blind sons along with him. The man bowed before the king and pleaded, "Your Majesty! I have lost everything in my business. I am in a difficult situation and I urgently need five hundred gold coins to pay my debts. Please, be kind enough to lend me this money O' King. I promise to repay you the amount within a short period of time."

He continued and said, "My Lord! I will leave my two sons with you as a guarantee against the loan. They will be at your service. They are extremely intelligent and talented."

The king looked very surprised and said, "How can two blind persons be of any use to me."

"Sir! please don't look down upon them," answered the old man. "Their blindness is no handicap to their talent. My elder son is very knowledgeable about horses and the second one is an expert jewel appraiser. They would serve you well, O King," said the old man.

The king was still not convinced. "I find it difficult to believe that blind people can undertake such work," he said.

The old man assured him, "Your Majesty! My sons have the power to know things just by smell and touch. If you feel that their sense of judging is wrong, you can behead them or you can even punish them suitably." The king agreed to this suggestion and handed over five hundred gold coins to the old man. The blind brothers were appointed in the service of the king.

Few days passed. One day, a horse trader brought a horse for sale. The trader while explaining its good qualities to the king claimed that the horse was of a foreign breed. The king got lured by the trader's words, wanted to buy the horse. So, he asked the blind brother to examine the horse and give his opinion.

The horse trader commented, "O' King, don't you think we are wasting our time in asking a blind person to examine the horse." Not listening to the trader, the king ordered the blind boy to examine the horse.

The blind boy touched the horse's body gently with his fingers. Later he touched the horse's legs and felt something. He turned towards the king and said, "My Lord! I would advice you not to buy the horse. You will not be able to ride it well." The trader got very angry with the eldest blind brother. He demanded that the king should have the horse tested. The king called upon his ace horse rider and ordered him to take a test-ride. As the rider was about to mount the horse, it threw him off. The trader was dismayed. "The horse has never behaved in this manner with me," he said.

The blind boy retorted, "Yes, it will never harm you. You are a milkman. Why did you give up your job as the milkman?" he asked in an amused tone.

"How did you know that previously I worked as a milkman," asked the trader in surprise. The blind boy replied, " The horse is not of a foreign breed. It was born in your stable. Infact, both its parents are also with you. You have been feeding the horse with buffalo's milk. I could ascertain all these facts by the scent of the horse." The trader had to accept that he was trying to cheat the king and left the king's court in a huff. The king felt happy to have such a knowledgeable person in his service.

A few days later, a jeweller came to the king's court with the intention of selling some of his precious gems. The king selected a large gem and asked the younger blind brother to assess its value. The blind boy rubbed the gem between his palms and told the king, "Sir, it is definitely a valuable gem. But it is not a lucky stone. Therefore, whoever buys it, they will get ruined in their life."

The king turned towards the jeweller to find out if it was true. The jeweller was already pale and his hands were trembling with fear. The king on seeing the jeweller realised that he was a cheat and the blind boy was absolutely right in assessing the gem.

Many weeks passed. One morning, the father of these blind boys returned to the king's court and after repaying the loan of five hundred gold coins, he sought the king's permission to take his sons back.

The king asked him, "Yours sons are indeed intelligent and knowledgeable. You being the father of them, what is your talent?" The old man had the rare talent of recognising the truth of a man's birth.

The king was curious to test this statement. "What do you know about my birth?" he asked the old man. Without even hesitating, he replied, "Your ancestors were butchers." The king got angry at the old man's reply and ordered the old man and his sons to be put to death.

Betal's narration came to an end but he had the inevitable question. "Vikram! Tell me, the king had three lives killed. Who was responsible for the death of the old man and his sons?" "Listen, Betal!" replied vikram, "The king could not be blamed. He was a butcher's son and so inherited a butcher's traits. That is why he did not hesitate to kill somebody. The old man himself was responsible for his sons and his own death," explained Vikram further. "He need not have disclosed the truth about the king's birth. He created a pit for himself and his sons."

Betal praised King Vikram's reasoning. But since Vikram could not keep quiet, Betal sprang back to his favourite tree. Vikram ran behind him once again.

The Test

Having now accepted his frequent visits to the tamarind tree where Betal resides, as a part of his daily routine, King Vikram once again went to Betal, brought him down and carried him on his shoulders, and started walking. Betal had yet another story to tell.

Malayaketu was the king of Benares. He and his queen were always worried because they did not have children. After severe penance and ardent prayer, a daughter was born to them. They named her Rajeshwari. When she grew up, the king wanted to have her married to the best of bridegrooms. So he made an announcement in the kingdom and sent words for an eligible bachelor for his daughter. He also obtained various pictures of suitable princes so that Rajeshwari could choose a groom of her liking. She felt that she

could not decide on anyone of them by merely looking at the pictures. So she left the decision to her parents. She also told them that she wished to marry someone who was intelligent and brave.

The news that Rajeshwari wanted to marry an intelligent and brave man spread far and wide. Many suitors came to Benares to gain her hand in marriage. Out of these, one was a weaver. He claimed he could weave five fine clothes a day. "I donate one such cloth to the God, the second is given to a Brahmin and the other three will be used by me to run my family," he boasted.

Another suitor was a trader. He said that he could understand the language of all the beasts and birds. He claimed that the birds and beasts talk to him in a sign language and that he could relate to their woes and happiness.

The king and his daughter were amazed at such talents. An other suitor came to the king's court, the next day. He was a warrior. He was an ace swordsman and had successfully fought many battles. The fourth one was a brahmin. He said that he could make even the dead come alive with his knowledge.

All the four suitors were handsome and intelligent. Neither the king nor the princess could decide whom to select as the bridegroom.

Betal ended the story and asked the king. "Vikram! I have a doubt. Only you are capable of answering the question. Whom should Princess Rajeshwari marry? You know what will happen if you remain silent."

After a brief thought, King Vikram replied, "Dear Betal! you are forcing me to talk. And as soon as I open my mouth, you jump back

to the tree. I am sure you know the answer to the question you just asked."

Vikram continued to say, "After all, Princess Rajeshwari, being the king's daughter belongs to the warrior's clan. So it is very natural that she should marry someone from her own community. Moreover, she has specified that her husband should be a brave man. The weaver, the trader and the brahmin are not brave people, whereas the warrior has already proved his bravery by waging many wars. No doubt all the four princes were talented. But only the prince who was a warrior would win Princess Rajeshwari's hand in marriage. How can Rajeshwari be happy with a husband who can understand the language of the beasts; or with some one who can weave fine clothes? The brahmin seems to be a magician. So, in my opinion, O Betal, King Malayaketu should choose the warrior for his daughter."

"Your choice is the same as King Malayaketu's choice. And your way of judgement is indeed praiseworthy. But since you have spoken. I can't be of any help to you. I am bound with the condition that if you open your mouth and utter even a single word I shall escape from your clutches. So, here I go...." Betal got another opportunity to escape from Vikram's grasp.

The Noblest of All

By this time, Vikram has decided that he would overtake Betal in reaching the tree. So he ran very fast and even before Betal could reach the tree, caught him by the leg and pulled him down. Putting the corpse on his shoulders, Vikram started walking.

As he was walking, he stumbled against a stone and faltered. Betal thought that Vikram was feeling tired. So, he said gleefully, "Vikram, you look exhausted. So why don't you just send me back to the tree? You need not have to fulfil the promise you made to the sage."

Vikram did not make any reply. So, Betal tried his usual trick of telling a story. "This story is so interesting," he said, "It will lessen the tediousness of the journey."

Once, there was a trader called Rajdutt. He had a daughter by name Vanishri. When she grew up, her father thought of getting her married to an eligible young man who will look after her very well. Many days passed, another trader who was Rajdutt's friend came to visit him. He started talking about his son, Paramvir to Rajdutt. Rajdutt thought, "Here I find a groom for my daughter." The two friends spoke and the marriage was fixed. Vanishri got married to Paramvir.

Since Rajdutt could not bear the thought of being far away from his beloved daughter, he requested Paramvir, his son-in-law to come and live in his own house. Vanishri was the only daughter to Rajdutt. Paramvir agreed to this request.

Since Paramvir had come to live in her father's house, Vanishri hated her husband. She was filled with anger for him. She started disliking her husband even though Paramvir would not scold her for her behaviour

towards him. He thought, "She is quite immature, it will take time for her to adjust to a married lifestyle." Thinking that he kept all his feelings to himself.

Paramvir, however, was not aware of his wife's feelings. One day he went to his hometown to meet his parents. It took several days for him to return.

Meanwhile, Vanishri was glad to be alone. One evening, she sat in the balcony to get some fresh air. Many people were walking in the street. Out of them, a handsome young man by name Sudhakar caught her eye. It was love at first sight for both of them. They both kept looking at each other without blinking their eyes. Sudhakar stood in front of the balcony for sometime and departed from there with his friends.

Vanishri got back to her room thinking about Sudhakar. She could not sleep at nights and not eat in the day thinking only of Sudhakar. She had gone pale. Several days passed. Unable to bear the agony of love, Vanishri tried to commit suicide in her backyard.

Luckily for her, one of her maids spoiled her attempts to commit suicide. Sobbing on the maid's shoulders, Vanishri told her all about her futile love for Sudhakar. The maid took pity on her, consoled her and promised to bring Sudhakar to the nearby garden, the next day evening.

Sudhakar was also hoping to see Vanishri and express his love for her. Just as he was expressing his desire to meet her while talking to his friends, Vanishri's maid came running towards them. On reaching there, she enquired about Sudhakar. She told him of Vanishri's deteriorating condition and asked him to meet her in the city garden that evening.

Vanishri was overjoyed when she heard that Sudhakar is coming to the garden to meet her. At the specified hour, he reached the spot indicated by Vanishri's maid. The maid took him to Vanishri. She was waiting for Sudhakar by the tree near the pond and the maid left them and went away from there.

As soon as Vanishri saw Sudhakar, she came running to him and hugged him tightly. She was feeling extremely happy. Her happiness was so intense that she died in his arms. Sudhakar on seeing his love no more, stood stunned. He put her on his lap and shedding tears for his beloved's death, he also collapsed and died on the spot.

The night passed and Rajdutt was searching for his daughter. When the gardener opened the gates of the city garden next morning, he found two dead bodies in tight

embrace. The news reached Rajdutt and he came running to the garden.

On that particular day Paramvir also decided to return to his in-law's house. When he heard the news, he immediately went to the garden. The sight of his wife, dead with another man, was shocking. He could not bear the grief and he also died broken hearted.

Rajdutt who was a great devotee of Goddess Chandrika prayed before her to restore life to these three. His prayer was answered and all of them woke up as if from sleep. All those who had assembled there for the cremation and Rajdutt's relatives were happy to see them back with life.

Rajdutt advised his daughter to treat her husband well and took them home. Sudhakar felt ashamed of his behaviour and went away from the city.

The noblest of all

Having told the story, Betal asked the king, "Vikram! I am sure you will have known what my question will be. But still, I will ask you. Amongst Vanishri, Paramvir and Sudhakar, whose love was the noblest?" If you do not reply despite knowing the answer, your head shall shatter into pieces." And became silent.

Vikram knew the answer and had to answer the question. So he said, "Her husband, Paramvir is the noblest of them all. Because, inspite of seeing his wife dead in another man's embrace, his love for her did not weaken. More than that he died because of his love for her. Undoubtedly Paramvir's love was supreme."

Laughing demonically Betal said, "Vikram, I knew you will answer the question correctly but you have talked! So. You know I have to go." Betal was next seen at the tamarind tree hanging upside down.

✪ ✪ ✪

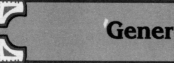

Just as Betal waited wondering whether the king, having decided that he wanted nothing more to do with the spirit, had returned to his kingdom as a result of which there would be no one to listen to the stories. King Vikram reached the tree. As always, the king brought Betal down and patting him across his shoulders, Vikram started walking.

"I am surprised at your desperate attempts to take me," said the Betal. He started narrating yet another story.

Hundreds of years ago, a king ruled Mythila. He was called Visakhadatta. He was a very generous king. Everyday he donated food, clothing and money to the poor in abundance. There is no measure to his generosity. Lakhs of rupees from the royal treasury were spent.

The king had a wise and loyal minister named Raghuveer. The minister was a very sensible man. He advised the king not to be overspending the money without any proper cause. "No doubt you are the most generous king amongst others, but if this goes on for a long time, you might end up losing everything in life O' King. Save for the future of this kingdom, My Lord. We need to be sensible about this," pleaded the minister. The king gave a deaf ear to Raghuveer's words and he continued doing the same thing. The king reasoned it by saying that he derives an immense pleasure and satisfaction in giving charity to the poor.

Time and again, the minister Raghuveer pleaded to the king to control giving his money away without bothering about the future. As days passed by, the king's deeds just increased. Raghuveer was not able to bear this. The

minister decided to leave the kingdom as the king did not pay any heed to his advice. "I am of no help to the king. I cannot see the king ruining his kingdom like this," thought Raghuveer. Getting upset with the king's attitude, the minister gave up his job and left the kingdom to a far off place.

Raghuveer kept wandering and reached the seashore the next morning. All of a sudden, there was a strange site. Raghuveer could not believed his eyes. An unusual island emerged out of the sea. On the island, there was a golden tree. The branches and leaves of the tree were glittering with precious gems and stones.

Raghuveer stood there in silence. He looked stunned and was amazed at the sight. As he stood there, he could see a beautiful maiden sitting under the golden tree. He jumped into the water and swam to the island. As he went near the tree, he could see stars sparkling around her. Raghuveer asked the maiden "Who are you?" "I belong to the serpent world situated on the sea bed," answered the girl. "I rise above the sea everyday to be in your world for some time. You look like a wise man to me. Can you help me? O noble man. I want to meet a king from your world," asked the girl.

Raghuveer said, "I know of a king who is very generous. I will bring him here so that you can meet him." The girl then offered Raghuveer plenty of gold and said, "Remember, you should use this gold only for selfless services." Raghuveer collected as much gold as he could from the tree and took leave of the maiden.

The next morning, Raghuveer returned to mythila. He then met the king and explained to him all that he had witnessed at the seashore. At first, the king laughed it off and did not

believe him. "The serpent girl has a secret wish to meet you O King. Why don't you come along with me, my Lord! That would be a great experience for you," suggested Raghuveer.

Next day morning, they left for the seashore. The whole day they travelled and reached the place in the evening. At the expected moment, the strange island emerged out of the sea. The king saw the charming maiden sitting under the sea. "Is this some kind of a magic...I don't believe this," the king wondered. He jumped into the sea and swam upto the serpent girl.

Raghuveer waited at the shore. "O kind lady, I have come to meet you. I am the king of Mythila," said the king as he walked up to the golden tree. He continued, "If you are kind enough to offer the gold from the tree, I promise I will use it only for the betterment of my people." On hearing this, the serpent girl sprang up and cheered, "You are a king. How long I have been waiting to meet a king." On saying this, she fell at the king's feet. The king felt sorry for the girl and asked her, "What do you want from a king, O kind lady?"

"I am a daughter of a serpent. A demon has got hold of me with his evil powers. He wants a kingdom in return for my freedom. My father is not able to fulfil the demon's demand. I will be released from his clutches if you give away your kingdom. Please help me O' King," pleaded the girl.

Feeling sorry for the maiden and the king also liked her charm, he readily agreed to donate his entire kingdom to the demon for the sake of the girl. He released her from the demon and his evil spell. Just then the maiden came to her actual self and revealed the truth. "O kind king, I am actual a serpent princess. I was destined to marry the most generous and kind- hearted king in the world. You happened to be the most generous and I have been waiting for you for a long time. A vast kingdom and endless wealth is waiting for you down the sea. Come with me, O King," she said happily.

The king and the princess then dived into the water holding each other's hands. They never returned. Meanwhile, the minister Raghuveer was waiting at the seashore for the king. He waited endlessly and there was no sign of the king. Even after several days, the king did not come back. Raghuveer ended his life in disgust.

Betal tapped on Vikram's shoulder and said, "Vikram, the story ends here. But tell me, who was responsible for the loyal minister's death?" King Vikram replied, "Minister Raghuveer was responsible for his own death. If he was loyal, he should have never left his job. Then he would not have discovered the strange island. He gave king the opportunity to meet the maiden knowing very well that the king was very generous. The king would not have met the maiden and donated his entire kingdom. Raghuveer's mistake gave rise to the sequence of events and at last ended his life."

Betal agreed with King Vikram's answer. But once again he got the reason to fly back to the tamarind tree. King Vikram, as usual, started chasing the Betal.

The Honest Thief

Vikram pulled down Betal once again from the tree. With the determination to take Betal to the sage, he walked briskly in total silence. Betal tried to make conversation with him but finding Vikram absolutely tight lipped, he narrated a story.

Hundreds of years ago, there lived a king called Amarnath, in the kingdom of Avanti. He had a parrot by name Thotaram. Thotaram was very talkative. The parrot had visited many places and many kingdoms. The King Amarnath loved Thotaram very much and he took good care of him. One day, as he was talking to Thotaram, he asked, "My dear Thotaram, you have travelled far and near. There is no place or sea where you have not been. You have been to many kingdoms and probably seen many princesses. Why don't you suggest a princess who is suitable for me and be a good wife to me?"

The parrot asked the king to give him sometime. The next day, Thotaram proposed the name of Rajeshwari, who happened to be the princess of Magadha. There were only praises for the princess from Thotaram. The king at once sent his messengers to Magadha asking for princess' hand in marriage.

The princess of Magadha was also fond of pets. She had a pigeon. "Amarnath, the king, of Avanti is the ideal husband for you," advised the pigeon to its mistress. Princess Rajeshwari now wanted to see the king and had developed a soft corner for him.

Her father, the king of Magadha was also very happy to receive Amarnath's proposal. He immediately agreed to the wedding.

Amarnath and Rajeshwari had a grand wedding conducted on an auspicious day.

Meanwhile, the parrot and the pigeon became good friends and shared the same cage. They had the same likings. They talked to each other a lot and were very comfortable in each other's company.

The pigeon was very impressed with the widely travelled parrot. "I would like you to tell me an interesting incident that actually happened," the pigeon requested.

Thotaram narrated the following incident. In the city of Manipur, there lived a rich trader called Ramabhadra. He was a very wise and kindhearted man. But his wife was exactly the opposite. She was ill-tempered and had no morals. She behaved badly with others. The people of the city pitied Ramabhadra. They had a daughter named, Prabhavati.

Unfortunately, when Prabhavati grew up, she also followed her mother's footsteps. Ramabhadra was very worried for her daughter. He felt that marriage would reform Prabhavati. So he had her married

immediately. But even marriage did not improve Prabhavati in any way. She did the same things and her bad habits continued.

As her father was worried, he wanted to know how Prabhavati was behaving with her husband, he sent his servant to Prabhavati's house to check on her. This servant had been Prabhavati's lover before she got married.

On seeing the servant coming to her house, she panicked and thought, "What will happen if my husband comes to know of my love affair with this servant. He will definitely throw me out of his house. She quickly thought of a plan." She offered milk, which was poisoned by her to the servant. Not knowing about Prabhavati's wicked plan, he drank the milk. The servant was dead within minutes.

Prabhavati quickly hid the body in the room. In the evening, her husband returned home after his usual day's work. In the night while her husband was fast asleep. She started screaming "Help, Help! My husband has killed my father's servant by poisoning him."

Awakened by her shouts, all the neighbours rushed to Prabhavati's house. Her husband was shocked on seeing his wife's behaviour. He pleaded with the crowd, "Do not punish me. I am innocent, I know nothing about this." But there was no one who heard him and they had him arrested.

During the trial, the king also believed what Prabhavati said and sentenced her husband to death on charges of murdering the servant.

This news had spread all over the kingdom. Luck favoured Prabhavati's husband in the form of a thief. The thief also happened to hear this news. He got quite disturbed. On that particular night, the thief happened to be in Prabhavati's house to rob the valuables and he overheard the conversation between Prabhavati and her father's servant.

He was also witness to the fact that it was Prabhavati who added the poison to the milk.

Knowing about the punishment given to Prabhavati's husband, he went straight to the king and told him the truth. He also admitted that he had gone to Prabhavati's house to commit a theft.

After listening to the thief, the king released Prabhavati's husband from the prison. Instead, Prabhavati was sentenced to death. He also praised the thief for his courage and honesty. "You spoke the truth and saved an innocent life. You are really a brave man. I will forgive all the crimes you have committed since you have been honest about it," the king said.

Vikram heard this story within a story in total silence. Betal asked, "Vikram, who was the guilty person in this entire incident."

"Betal, the thief was an honest person. By telling the truth to the king at the appropriate time, he saved Prabhavati's husband from death. In fact, it was Ramabhadra, Prabhavati's father who was truly the guilty person," replied Vikram

"Why do you say that?" asked Betal.

"Ramabhadra knew fully well that his daughter was not of good character. He did not reveal these facts to Prabhavati's husband at the time of marriage. He was not bothered about the man who will wed his daughter. Her husband suffered because of Prabhavati's conduct. That is why Ramabhadra is guilty of dishonesty," explained Vikram in a logical manner.

"You are truly an amazing and intelligent person, great King," applauded Betal just before flying back to his haunted tree.

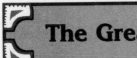

The Greatest Sacrifice

Vikram ran as fast as he could and catching hold of the corpse, pulled it down. Then, putting it across his shoulders, he started walking towards the place where the sage was waiting for him. Betal was amused to find Vikram so desperate. And to make him break the silence, Betal began his story as follows...

Once a king named Jimut had a son called Jimutavahan. His son had many good qualities in him and all the citizens of the kingdom praised him for his generosity and benevolence. He respected his elders and teachers showed a lot of concern for the poor people and animals.

In the backyard of the king's palace, there was a wishing tree, Kalpavriksh. The tree had the powers to fulfil all desires. One day, as Jimutavahan was standing under the wishing tree, he thought, "I wish, there is only happiness

and prosperity bestowed upon one and all in this kingdom." Soon, the tree grew taller and taller and its branches spread to every corner of the kingdom, Jimutavahan's wish was granted. Throughout the kingdom, it showered precious gems and stones everywhere. And thus the people became richer and there was no place for sorrow. They all had praises for Jimutavahan and prayed for him for eliminating poverty in the land. The king also admired his son for his gesture.

But, on the other hand, his relatives were very jealous of him. They wanted to overthrow him by waging war. When Jimutavahan heard of this plan, he went to his father and said, "Father, let our relatives rule the kingdom. We should not wage a war just for the sake of this worldly existence. We will live in a calm, peaceful atmosphere faraway from here and serve the people through our noble deeds."

Jimutavahan made his father realise the deeper significance of the philosophy of life and gave up his kingdom without causing any bloodshed. Jimutavahan took his parents to Malaya mountains. They built a small hut with their own hands and started living life like hermits.

Shortly afterwards, Jimutavahan met another young man by name Keshav and a friendship developed between them. Keshav had a sister called Parvathi. Jimutavahan saw her once in a temple offering prayers. He fell in love with her. She also liked Jimutavahan. With the permission of the elders, they were married on an auspicious day.

Jimutavahan and Parvathi would often stroll on the nearby beach, enjoying each others company.

Once, they spotted a heap of bones. He was aghast at this sight. He immediately rushed to his friend, Kehav and asked him, "Keshav!

Do you know anything about the heap of bones just behind the shore?" "Yes, my friend", replied Keshav. "These are bones of millions of Nagas (serpents) killed by Garuda, the king of eagles. Vasuki, the king of Patala sends them one by one for Garuda to eat. Everyday one Naga is to be sent to Garuda to become his food."

Jimutavahan felt distressed at the thought that being a king, Vasuki was handing over his subjects to the enemy one by one, "How could a king be so selfish" he wondered.

Jimutavahan couldn't resist visiting the same spot the next day. Just then, he saw a young being brought as the eagle's food for the day. Behind him was his mother wailing. He is my only son. Is there nobody who could save my son." Jimutavahan's heart was moved. He told her, "Please do not worry. When Garuda comes, I will offer myself in place of your son. Nothing will happen to your son."

Both the mother and the son did not agree to Jimutavahan's plan. But Jimutavahan insisted on his offer and stood on the death rock waiting for Garuda.

Shortly afterwards Garuda swooped on Jimutavahan and picking him up in his claws, took him to Malaya mountains. Just as the eagle king was about to eat him Jimutavahan cried, "May my life be utilized for the welfare of the human race in all my re-births!"

On hearing this, Garuda suddenly realised that this was not an ordinary Naga but a great soul. Now it so happened that while being taken away by Garuda, Jimutavahan's ring had slipped out of his finger and fell on the ground near his hut. Parvathi recognized her husband's ring and came running to the place where Garuda was all set to eat Jimutavahan. At the same time, the young Naga boy had also ran after Garuda. Seeing the eagle king, he shouted, "O' Garuda. The one in your clutches is Jimutavahan, a divine person. I am a Naga. Please eat me up." But by now it was too late. Jimutavahan's blood flowed out of his body and he was dead.

Seeing her husband dead, Parvathi prayed to the Goddess Gauri to make him come alive. The Goddess heard the prayer and descending to earth, sprinkled some holy water on Jimutavahan to get back his life.

Pleased with Jimutavahan's sacrifice and greatness, Garuda wanted to grant him a boon. Jimutavahan said, 'O Garuda, Henceforth, please do not kill any Naga. I do not want anything for myself. Let all those eaten up by you until now be alive."

Garuda brought some nectar from the heaven and sprinkled it on the heaps of bones. All the dead Nagas were soon alive. Garuda never killed anybody again.

Betal ended the story and asked Vikram, "Tell me, O King, whose sacrifice was the greatest and the noblest, the young Naga boy's or Jimutavahan's? "It's the Naga boy's sacrifice, that is greater," replied King Vikram.

"How? After all, Jimutavahan was prepared to die for the Naga boy," asked Betal. "The acts of sacrifice and generosity were not new to Jimutavahan. He was born a noble soul and so it was natural to him to save the boy from Garuda's clutches. On the other hand, the Naga boy offered his body as food. He was from an ordinary background. And he had escaped from death. This was truly sacrifice. That is why the Naga boy was the most benevolent of the two," replied Vikram.

"You are right again great King but since your silence has been broken I am going back to the tree," said Betal and flew back to his favourite tamarind tree.

True Love

Betal as usual began narrating a story. Once upon a time, there lived a king by name Jagat Pratap. He ruled a city called Madharpur. The king loved his subjects very much. He cared for their sorrows and fulfilled their needs. The king had a close friend called Ramsagar. He was a rich trader in the same city. Ramsagar had a daughter, Ratna. Her father wanted Ratna to get married to a suitable boy. He began searching for an eligible bachelor. But Ratna did not like anybody. She decided that she would choose her husband at the right time and inform her father about him.

Ramsagar, being a lovable father, did not force Ratna into marriage and left the choice to her.

Meanwhile, there was a thief in the city who had everybody's attention. Every night,

he committed a theft. He was so clever that people were unable to catch him. They all spent sleepless nights thinking that the thief would rob their house that night. The entire city lived in fear. It became so unsafe that some people even left the city. The king was worried and had thought of several plans to catch hold of the thief but in vain. He had his security service tightened to have this thief arrested at any cost. The people of his kingdom pleaded to the king to remedy the situation.

After all this, his men failed to catch the thief. He himself wanted to do something. He disguised himself like a commoner and wandered through the streets of the city in the night when the thief was active. On one such night, he saw a man jumping over the wall of a house.

The king immediately ordered his men to catch the person. The guards, very cautiously caught him when the thief was about to leave the house after a theft. He had with him all the stolen articles from the house which was proof enough to identify him as a thief.

The king felt relieved. The thief was chained and paraded in the street so that the people of the city could heave a sigh of relief. Ratna, Ramsagar's daughter happened to see the thief when he passed her house. She immediately fell in love with him. The thief was a handsome young man and Ratna was attracted to him. She ran to her father said, 'O Father, "you have always wanted me to get married. I have decided to listen to you. I want to marry the thief. Please speak to the king and have him released."

On hearing this, Ramsagar was upset that his daughter wanted to marry a thief. But he could not do anything at all. "If the thief is hanged, I will jump into the fire I have accepted

him as my husband," said Ratna. She was very adamant.

Having no choice left, he went to the king and said, "Your majesty I am in a difficult situation. My daughter wants to get married to the thief arrested last night. I tried to make her understand that this would be foolish. But she does not listen to me. Please have the thief released."

The king was shocked to hear this. "This is not possible, my friend, If I have him released, the people will lose faith in me and the thief will continue to commit thefts. He must be hanged," said the king.

"My daughter will jump into the funeral pyre and end her own life. I love my daughter very dearly. For the sake of my friendship with you, kindly spare the thief," pleaded Ramsagar. The king refused.

Very dejected, Ramsagar returned and again advised Ratna to change her mind. But she did not listen. By this time news had spread among the people that a rich and beautiful girl like Ratna actually wanted to marry a thief, when the thief heard about this, he wept bitterly.

On the day of execution, the thief was taken to the market in the centre of the city. A platform had been built there to hang him by the neck. All the citizens of the city had gathered there to watch the thief die. It would mean an end to their nightmare.

Ratna had lit up a large fire next to the platform where the thief was to be hanged. She declared before the crowd that she had accepted the thief as her husband and like a true wife, she was committing 'sati' (jumping into the fire on the death of the husband). On hearing this, the thief roared with laughter.

Shortly afterwards the thief was hanged to death. Ratna also jumped into the fire and committed Sati.

Betal ended his narration. "Vikram! I find the entire story very strange. I am puzzled by the thief's behaviour. Can you tell me why the thief wept bitterly at first and later on roared with laughter? What could be the reason?" he asked.

Vikram was ready with his reply, "Betal, if you analyse the thief's behaviour you will not find it strange. It was evident that an intelligent person like him could have escaped. When he came to know that Ratna loved him, he wished that she should have come into his life before be became a thief. This made him cry bitterly. As against this, he was amused that Ratna, who had not even been married to him, is all set to commit suicide. This filled him with laughter," was Vikram's explanation.

But inspite of Vikram breaking his silence, Betal did not fly back to the tree. King Vikram was very surprised. Betal smiled at him an said, "Vikram! Now this time, I am not going back to the tamarind tree."

Vikram quickened his pace and reached the place indicated by the sage where he was waiting for both of them patiently. Just before reaching the place, Betal warned Vikram, "The sage is evil. He wants to sacrifice both of us to attain more mystical powers. He intends to chop your head when you bow low before him." Vikram did not respond to what the Betal said.

The sage saw King Vikram with the Betal and was delighted. He thanked Vikram. Then the sage cut Betal into pieces and threw them into the burning fire. Vikram was watching what the sage did. Then the sage turned to Vikram and asked him to bow before the fire